George and Matilda Mouse and the Doll's House
first published 1988
George and Matilda Mouse and the Floating School
first published 1990

This edition published 1994 by Dean
in association with Methuen Children's Books
an imprint of Reed Consumer Books Ltd
Michelin House, 81 Fulham Road, London SW3 6RB
and Auckland, Melbourne, Singapore and Toronto

ISBN 0 603 55223 4

Printed in Italy by Olivotto

TALES OF
GEORGE and MATILDA
MOUSE

HEATHER S. BUCHANAN

DEAN

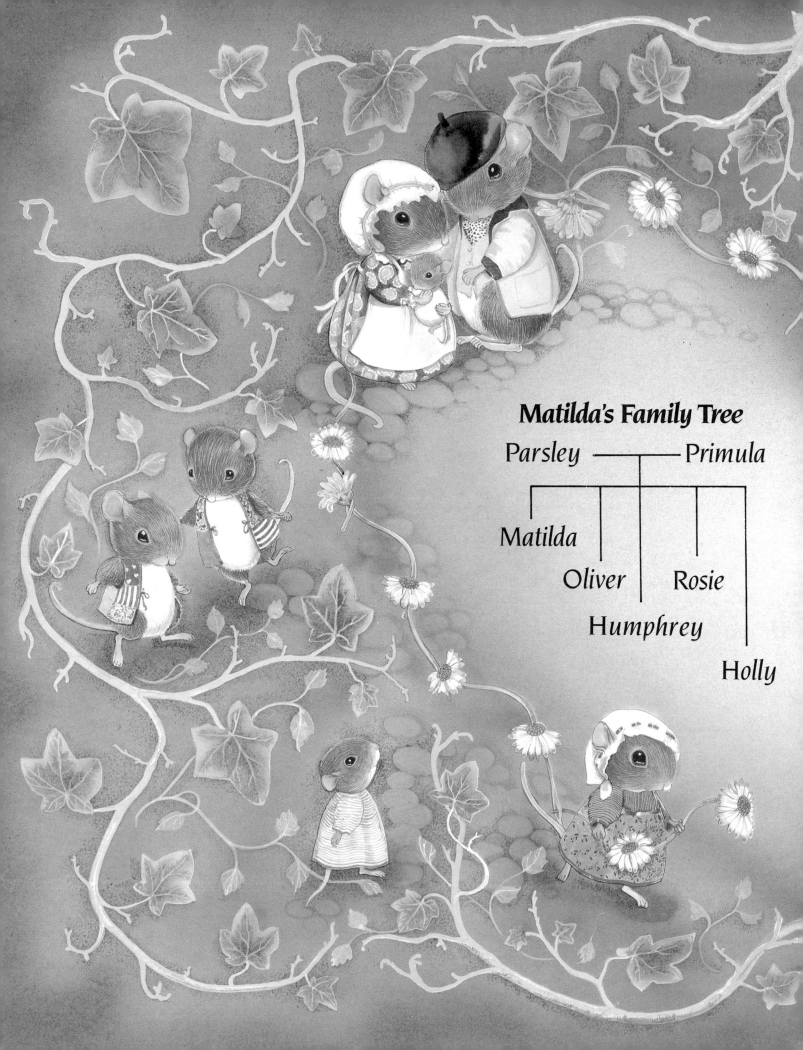

Matilda's Family Tree

Parsley ——————— Primula

Matilda

Oliver

Humphrey

Rosie

Holly

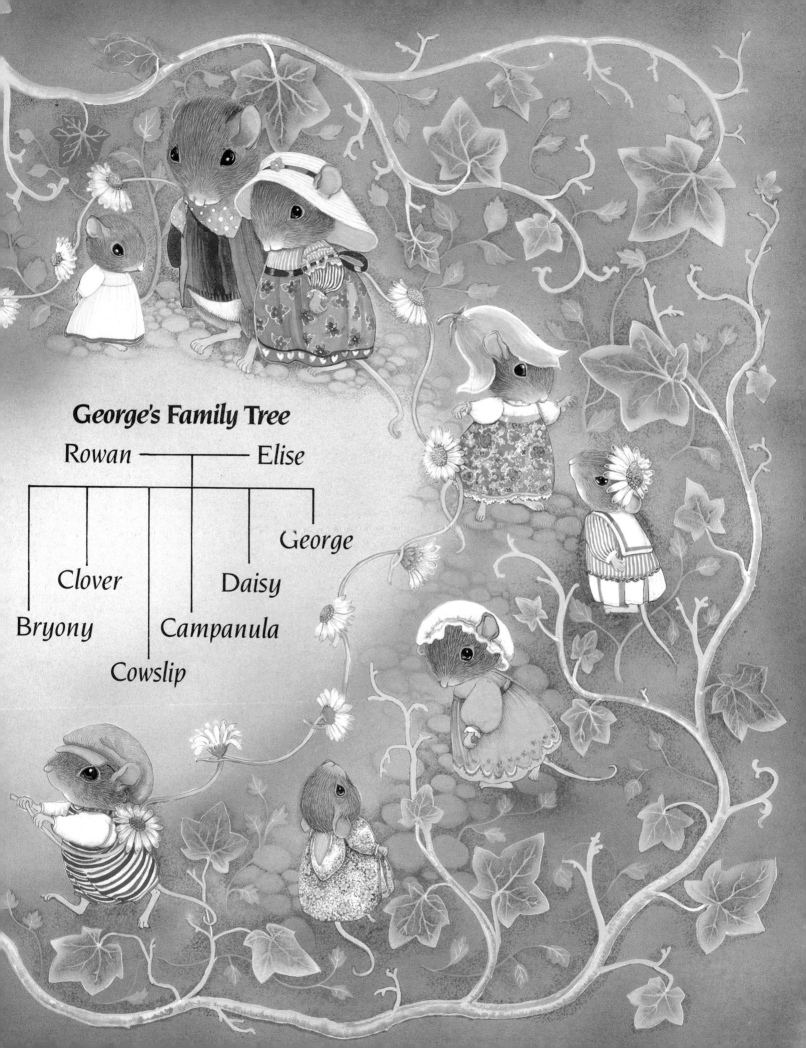

George's Family Tree

Rowan ——————— Elise

Bryony

Clover

Cowslip

Campanula

Daisy

George

For all the great-grandchildren
of Elsie Wetherall Hart (1888-1984)
who bought the Dolls' House
for her daughter in the 1920's,
who then gave it to the author
when she was a little girl,
and then George and Matilda moved in.

GEORGE AND MATILDA MOUSE
and the
DOLLS' HOUSE

It was a very special day. This was the day George and Matilda Mouse were to be married at Tree Stump House. George's mother was icing the wedding cake and his sister Bryony was making trifles and arranging the food on the table. Clover and Cowslip were weaving a reed basket for George, which he was soon going to use to fetch Matilda, travelling by inflatable balloon.

George's youngest sisters Daisy and Campanula were sent out to find flowers to make into garlands to hang across the windows and down the staircase of Tree Stump House. Everyone rushed around and felt excited. Especially George.

George had found the balloon caught high in a tree several weeks ago and had climbed up to rescue it, carefully letting the air out of it so that it did not burst. When he got it home all the mice took turns at blowing it up to test its strength.

Now they all puffed into it again and it began to billow out into a lovely round shape. They tied its mouth securely to keep all the air in. Then they harnessed it with grasses woven into rope above the reed basket, which they had decorated with forget-me-nots.

When the wind direction was just right, the balloon lifted up into the air and George took off, sailing up and over the trees. He was soon floating away on the breeze, towards the sea.

Matilda had been up since dawn, brushing her whiskers and dabbing behind her ears with rose water. Oliver and Humphrey, her twin younger brothers, had been up early too and had found her some rockroses to use as a headdress. She saved two to put behind Rosie's ears. Rosie was her little sister, and she loved dressing up.

Matilda and her family lived in a teapot in a cottage. They were house mice. Today Matilda was travelling into the country to marry George who was a field mouse. They had met whilst he was on holiday near her home. A sandcastle house she was making had collapsed on top of her and George had pulled her out. They had become great friends.

Matilda had a wonderful wedding dress, made from lace her father had found on a petticoat belonging to the old lady in their cottage. He had nibbled it off while she was asleep. Matilda's mother helped him turn it into a dress, with enough left over for a trailing veil too.

With the rockroses on her head, and splendid in the beautiful dress, Matilda stood with her family on the beach, watching the sky for George. They had been waiting quite a long time and Rosie kept skipping about so that her flowers fell off, and Matilda had to keep running after her to put them back.

As he floated along, George could at last see them all waving below him. Matilda's veil was streaming out in the wind. The little ones were jumping up and down and Matilda's mother was giving the baby a drink of milk.

George lowered the balloon by loosening the string and letting some of the air escape. When it was nearly empty the basket thudded down onto the sand and George climbed out. Greetings were exchanged and George and Matilda hugged each other. Then George showed them all where to sit in the basket and stowed away Matilda's suitcase. She had packed her trousseau in it, that is, all the things she had made for her new home with George. There was also a patchwork quilt, a shell George had given her, and her everyday apricot-coloured dress rolled up in her headscarf.

When they were ready George began to blow up the balloon again, and Oliver and Humphrey helped. But the wind was still blowing out to sea so they weighted the basket with pebbles which prevented them from taking off. They sang a few songs whilst they waited for the wind to change. Then, when Matilda's veil blew towards the land, they all cheered, heaved the pebbles over the side and floated up and up, across the sand.

They drifted across a patchwork of fields and trees, until at last they arrived at Tree Stump House and saw stretching out beneath them a welcoming pathway of daisyheads.

The huge table had been covered with delicious cakes and puddings and nuts. There were garlands of flowers everywhere.

The mice climbed out, and George put on his best grey coat and top hat. Then the wedding began. Matilda took George's paw and they walked slowly to the bottom of the staircase, whilst Rosie held on to Matilda's veil. They all stood absolutely still, the bride and bridegroom in the middle and all the other mice in a circle around them. One old mouse began to sing an ancient mouse song about how mice lived and loved hundreds of years ago. Then all the others joined in, and the song bubbled and flowed like a stream, round and round the circle. All mice learn these special marriage songs.

At last the oldest mouse stepped forward. He took George's paw and placed Matilda's paw carefully on top, and then he wrapped a daisy stem right around them, to show that the mice hoped to stay together for ever. Then all the other mice stepped forward from the circle in turn, each carrying a little rush basket containing a small gift. Some brought acorns, some soapwort flowers for bathing, some little heart-shaped wedding biscuits and some special herbs to use as medicine and for cooking.

George's sisters picked up their instruments and played mouse country dance music. George and Matilda joined paws and all the others danced, weaving in and out of a daisy chain around them. When it was nearly dark the mice lit torches and George fetched his wedding present for Matilda from his secret workshop under the roots of Tree Stump House. It was a beautiful travelling cart.

Matilda settled herself comfortably inside and all the mice sang a special farewell song as the newly-wedded mice set off into the darkening woodland and began their search for a new home together.

They slept under the starry sky by a little stream, wrapped in Matilda's patchwork quilt. They breakfasted on wedding cake, and then continued their journey, finding a broad road and following it by creeping along under the hedgerows.

They had decided to go to the town to find a home. George liked inventing machines and he hoped to find useful things for making these in people's dustbins. Matilda loved exploring, and was longing to see a town.

As evening came they found that the houses they passed were getting closer together and that the ground under their feet was becoming very hard. They were amazed by the size and noise of the cars and lorries on the road, and they kept well in, close to the walls of the shops and buildings that they passed.

No one noticed the two small mice
as they stopped to gaze up at the
window of a greengrocer's shop.
The colours of the fruit and vegetables
looked like patchwork to Matilda.

They came finally to a battered garden gate with a hole underneath it, and George, who felt very tired, decided to stop. He pulled the cart under the gate and looked around him. They were at the bottom of a town garden and through the gathering dusk he could just see what he guessed was a dustbin. He was delighted.

Just beside their little cart was a large grey metal thing with a handle and spout. It was a watering can. George climbed up the side and peered in.

It looked warm and dry and would make a good place to spend the night, hidden from any cats. He quickly collected flowers, twigs and leaves and dropped them down inside. Then he lowered a ladder of daisychains and climbed down himself. He made a nest, decorated it with the flowers and fetched Matilda, who had fallen asleep wrapped in their quilt. She would have a lovely surprise, he thought, when she woke in the morning.

Matilda was indeed surprised when she woke. She was floating in a boat, with George snoring happily beside her. Above the watering can on the garage wall was a garden tap which must have been dripping all night. George and Matilda were now bobbing along in their nest, quite near to the spout opening in the can. Matilda woke George and they swam to the spout hole, pulling their patchwork quilt with them and using the lace train on her dress as a rope to tie themselves together with. They squeezed and squeezed up the spout and eventually popped out of the end like corks from a bottle. For a moment they lay shivering with fright in the grass below. Then quickly they collected Matilda's headscarf containing their everyday clothes and set off to search for a safer home.

They had hardly had time to look around them when they saw a moving shadow and realised as they caught her scent that there was a cat in the bushes. The two mice clung to each other and kept perfectly still, and at last dared to creep slowly into the dark ivy which spread along the wall nearby.

Feeling her way in the green darkness, Matilda's paw touched a small round handle, and at the same moment George tripped over a wooden step. They pulled away some of the ivy and discovered a tin door covered in spider's webs. Matilda pushed the door carefully open and they put their whiskers inside. Still fearful of the cat somewhere behind them they decided to go in, past the spiders and the ants. There was lots of dirt and dust. This was an old dolls' house that someone must have left here years and years ago. There was a kitchen with a table and a china-covered dresser, and there were already logs on the black cooking range. A caterpillar had been eating the curtains, but as their eyes grew accustomed to the darkness, the two mice knew that this could be the perfect home for them.

Before they dared to climb the stairs they squeaked together, to see if anyone was there. But there was no answer.

They found lots of spiders' webs on the landing, a tin bath and another door which opened into a bedroom. There was a hole in the ceiling and lots of dead leaves piled up on the iron bedstead. Again there were logs laid ready in the hearth, a dressing table with little drawers, and underneath it a doll's hat decorated with blue ribbon.

A ladder near the tin bath took them up once more, this time to an attic where they found a cot, a rocking horse and a wooden trunk full of tiny dolls and teddy bears. There was a Noah's Ark with all the animals lined up in pairs ready to go in.

George and Matilda sat down in the attic and thought hard. They did not know that they were in a doll's house and they were worried in case the owner of this lovely home might soon return. Perhaps they could just clean and tidy it for its owner whilst they made expeditions to the dustbin and remained safely hidden from the cat.

For the rest of the day the two mice tidied and cleaned. They began to feel very hungry and then remembered that they had left all their food in Matilda's suitcase in the cart by the watering can. George said he would go back after dark to fetch it.

They chased away the poor frightened spiders and earwigs, who were angry and didn't want to leave at all. The woodlice curled up and rolled away quickly when they saw Matilda coming with her doll's broom.

George got the fire going in the kitchen, and Matilda found a bucket with which she scooped up some water from a puddle outside. They washed and swept and scrubbed by the firelight until it was very dark.

Then George crept out and Matilda stoked up the fire so that its light
would guide him back through the ivy.

   He scurried along the wall, twitching his whiskers carefully to sense any
danger. He found the watering can easily because it was so large and grey,
and there beside it was his little cart. But to his horror he saw it was on its
side and a large black paw was patting it.

George froze. The moon slid out from behind the clouds and George saw the cat sniffing the mouse smell on the cart. But his scent was upwind and the cat had not seen him. He stayed deathly still and watched his cart being tapped and tossed into the air. He felt sure that the axles would break and the wheels would fall off.

Then from somewhere else came a calling and a tin plate banging against a stone step. The cat raised her head and ran to be fed. George sighed with relief.

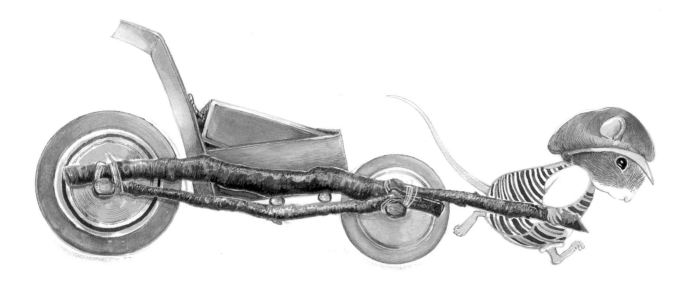

He ran as fast as he could and grabbed the cart, straightened it up, pushed the suitcase and their patchwork quilt into it and ran and ran, pulling it roughly behind him till he reached the dolls' house. He got terribly caught up in the ivy at first but he nibbled a pathway through the tendrils and was guided by Matilda's firelight glowing through the darkness.

George and Matilda were *so* glad to be safely back together again. They unpacked the remains of their wedding food and had a good supper in front of the fire. Then they fell asleep, wrapped in their quilt.

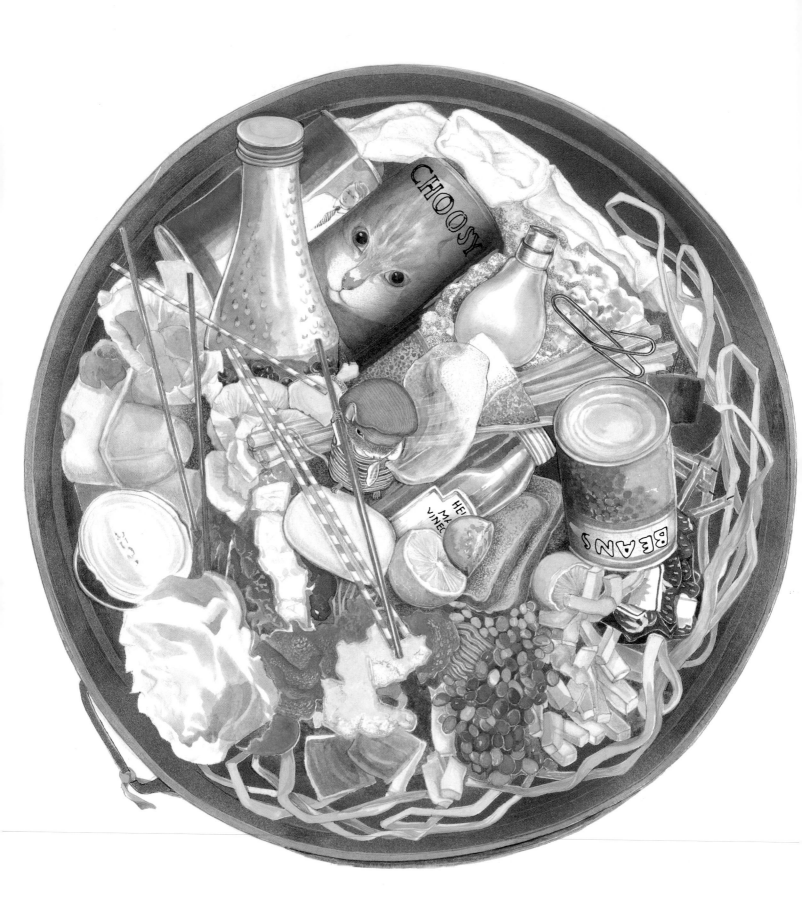

Next day it was time for their first dustbin adventure. Both mice crept out of the ivy, until they could see the dustbin beside the back door of the house. Then they had a tremendous piece of luck. The cat was shut in the house, gazing out of the window. She had not noticed them. If they moved quickly they could get the things they needed. They parked the cart by the dustbin and George inched his way up to the top. Then he squeezed under the ill-fitting lid and slipped down inside.

It was *terribly* smelly. But wonderful. There were dozens of useful things. He threw down to Matilda a piece of soap, a polythene bag, some silver foil, a selection of cheese-rinds, a few baked beans and some apple peel, four birthday cake candle stubs, a giant paper clip, some raffia and some scrunched-up paper. Matilda caught all these and packed them in the cart.

George slid down using some of his raffia, which he left attached to the handle for next time. Then they scurried away unseen, the cat still gazing out of the window and dreaming of a haddock breakfast.

Back home, they continued work on the dolls' house.

They boiled up more water and used the soap, nibbled into smaller pieces, to wash all the curtains and bedclothes they could find. They squeezed everything through the mangle (including George's tail by mistake, but he soon recovered!). He loved doing the washing because of all the bubbles. They heated up the old flat iron to press the curtains and they sewed them carefully together where the caterpillar had nibbled holes.

They polished the tiled floor, which shone like a horse-chestnut. They used the inside of sliced acorns to rub the wooden table and dresser and chairs, and soon these were shining too.

By the time darkness fell, all the linen was clean and airing, the fire in the bedroom was lit, and the two mice were sitting drinking acorn cocoa after a candlelit supper of a baked bean stuffed with cheese-rind crumbs, and for pudding sliced apple peel.

They cleaned their teeth with dolls' toothbrushes and then, feeling very tired but happy, they curled up in a clean bed wearing dolls' nightgowns for it was very cold.

The next day they made a list of jobs to do.

George went around the house calling out what needed to be done. HOLE IN ROOF. RICKETY CHIMNEY. LEAVES IN HINGES. Matilda wrote it all down. Then she went outside and called out what she found in the garden. PARSLEY. HERB-ROBERT. SCURVY GRASS. MINT. PLANT CARROTS. MAKE WATER PUDDLE BIGGER. George wrote all this down and they set to work.

The hole in the roof was the first job, and their polythene bag would be just perfect for that.

George had just started his climb to the roof by lassooing the chimney with rope when suddenly the mice heard a tapping on the tin front door.

They were very frightened. Could this be the real owner of the house?
Matilda slowly opened the door. There on the step was an old grey mouse
leaning on a walking stick, holding a bunch of daisies. 'To welcome you,'
he said. And then, when he looked past Matilda to the clean beautiful
kitchen, 'Well, well, well.'

Fergus Mouse did not own the dolls' house. He lived in an old boot
hidden in the ivy nearby. He was very old and wise. He could remember
the days when a little girl used to play with the dolls' house in the garden,
and he could remember her going away with her parents a long time ago,
and leaving the dolls' house behind.

He told George and Matilda all he knew about the garden. There was a beautiful rockery in the middle of the lawn under a lilac bush which had stood there for a hundred years. Beside the rockery lay a deep pond, and a stream trickled into it over the rocks, falling into the water from a stone scallop shell. Beneath the rocks and plants were hidden small doors to mouse homes and at night the eight mouse families living there crept out for parties and secret meetings. In the summer they splashed in the scallop shell and swam in the pond.

The mouse families needed a boat for travelling across the pond. They also needed someone to teach the children to read. George and Matilda looked at each other and smiled.

The year continued through late spring and into summer and the garden Matilda had created gave a good crop. Radishes did well and the carrots were enormous. Matilda had found a few seed packets which had been thrown into the dustbin and still had a few seeds left inside them.

George invented a special carrot harvesting machine and Fergus helped him to operate it.

By September they had made lots of raspberry jam and stored it in dolls' glass jars. They filled a nutstore at the back of the house, and stacked up lots of twigs, ready for the cold days. There was carrot wine laid down in plenty for special occasions.

Sometimes a passing bird carried a letter back to Tree Stump House or the teapot cottage, and occasionally Matilda was able to send her mother a special piece of cheese for the children or a beautiful scrap of material she had found in the dustbin. Letters were delivered to the dolls' house too, dropped like parachutes in the garden. It was good to have news of home.

Late in November Matilda and George had a marvellous piece of news to send. They thought that they would have babies of their own by Christmas.

Matilda had grown rounder and was often up in the attic choosing places for her babies to sleep, and imagining them playing with Noah's Ark.

On Christmas Eve, when Matilda was too round to fit easily into the rocking chair, George brought in a fir tree branch decorated with berries and hung with acorn lanterns for her and he set it in the centre of the kitchen.

Outside they could hear the rockery mice singing carols across the garden and snow was beginning to fall softly.

It was nearly midnight, so George helped Matilda up the stairs, and once she was in bed he went on up to make sure that no snow was coming in through the polythene patch on the roof.

When he returned, Matilda called him to come and see. There beside her on the pillow were five small pink mice, fast asleep. He touched each one very shyly. 'What a lovely Christmas,' he said, and put his paw gently round Matilda. Then he hung up seven dolls' socks at the foot of the bed, and all the mice slept.

As George made acorn tea in the morning, a passing robin dropped a parcel in the garden, so he hurried out into the snow to fetch it and put it under the Christmas tree.

The mouse family found lovely things in their stockings, a gold ring for Matilda, an oil stone for George to sharpen things with, and peanut rattles for the babies.

Then George trudged through the deep snow to Fergus's boot. He brought him back to share Christmas at the dolls' house and to see the babies.

When he arrived they all hugged each other and opened their parcels by the tree.

Fergus had a patchwork waistcoat, and he brought them a map of the garden, showing all the secret mouse houses. Matilda had a necklace George made by using coloured beads he found in the dustbin. She had made George a notebook in which he now proudly wrote down the names they had chosen for their babies.

Last of all they opened the parcel which the robin had brought, and found a knitted shawl from Matilda's mother and a snowdrop carefully wrapped in cotton wool, from her father.

Then they all had stilton cheese and carrot wine to celebrate their first wonderful Christmas in the dolls' house.

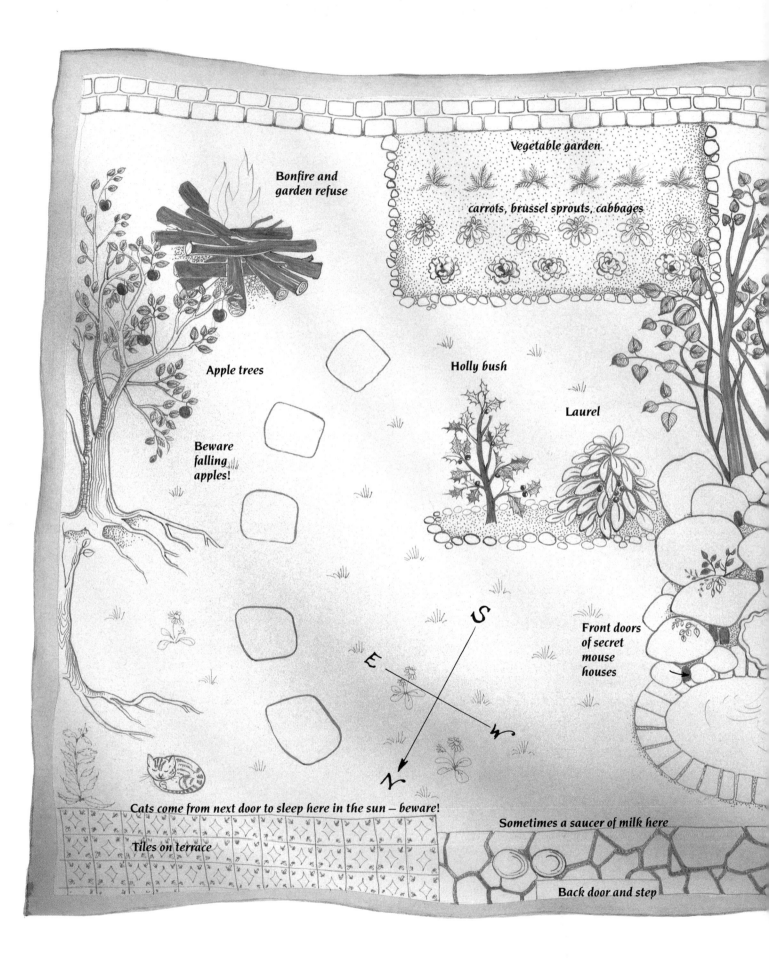

Bonfire and garden refuse

Vegetable garden

carrots, brussel sprouts, cabbages

Apple trees

Holly bush

Laurel

Beware falling apples!

Front doors of secret mouse houses

S

E

W

N

Cats come from next door to sleep here in the sun – beware!

Sometimes a saucer of milk here

Tiles on terrace

Back door and step

A map of the garden around the Dolls' House, drawn by Fergus Mouse

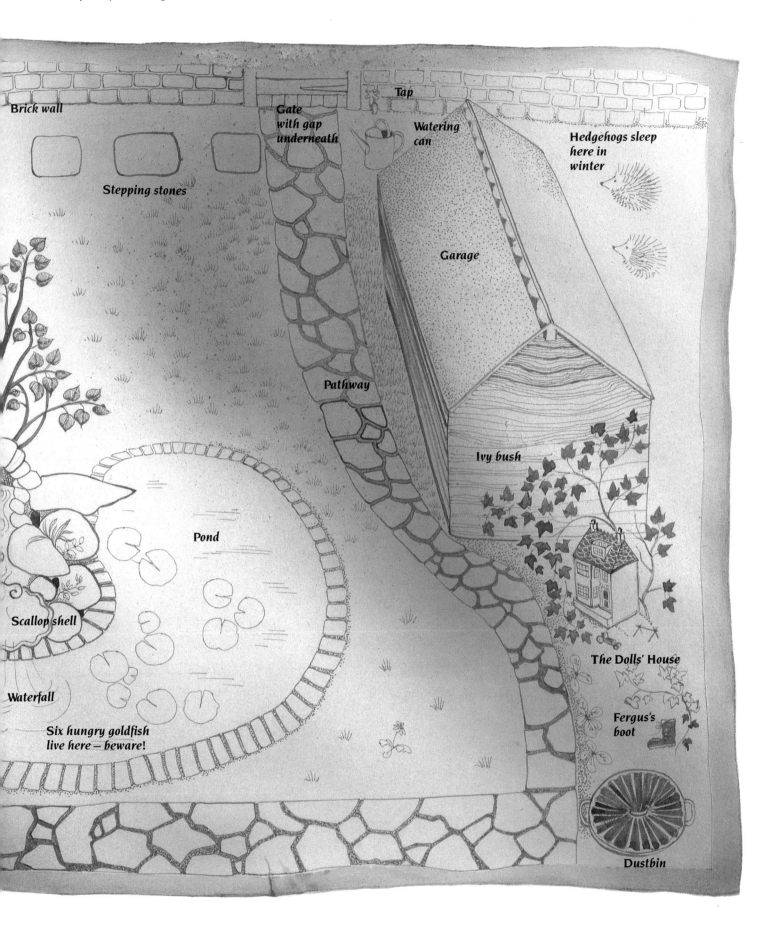

Brick wall

Stepping stones

Gate with gap underneath

Tap

Watering can

Hedgehogs sleep here in winter

Garage

Pathway

Ivy bush

Pond

Scallop shell

Waterfall

Six hungry goldfish live here – beware!

The Dolls' House

Fergus's boot

Dustbin

*To thank you all
for teaching my children*

George and Matilda Mouse
-and the-
Floating School

There was once a magnificent Dolls' House. It was tucked away in a dark corner of an old town garden.

Inside lived a family of seven mice – George and Matilda Mouse and their five children, Parsley, Mallow, Periwinkle, Columbine and Polyanthus. They were a cheerful, busy family who worked and played by night and slept by day.

The little mice were often very noisy, but inside the Dolls' House, with its glass windows and tin door they were safe from the cat, even when it could hear them squeaking.

But Matilda Mouse was worried. She wanted her children to play with other little mice. More than anything, she wanted them to go to school. She played Blind Man's Buff and Tig with them whenever she could and tried to teach them to read, but it was not the same as being in a proper school.

Suddenly Matilda knew what she must do. She would start her own school!

But a school needed pupils. A very old mouse, called Fergus, who lived nearby in a gardener's boot, had once told George and Matilda about the Rockery Mice. They lived under the rocks by a pond in the middle of the garden.

That night George and Matilda left their children with Fergus and set out to find the Rockery Mice.

Inside the mouse house a ladder of twigs led down into a light and wonderful burrow. There Matilda invited the little Rockery mice to come and learn their lessons with her own children in her new Dolls' House School.

The Rockery Mice were kind and clever garden mice. They already knew all the names and uses of plants in the garden. But they quickly agreed that school would be an excellent idea for their little mice. Lobelia, a grandmother mouse, promised to bring the first pupils the very next night.

The moon was shining brightly as Lobelia and a long line of little mice set out across the slippery rocks beside the pond, on the journey to school. All went well until Dandelion took an unwise leap over two rocks at once and fell, paws over tail, into the pond.

He splashed and squeaked frantically, terrified of the goldfish who lurked in the weeds. Then Lobelia lowered Lavender on her walking stick and she reached out and grabbed Dandelion just before the goldfish got him. Back on the rock Lobelia hugged him better and wrapped him warmly in her shawl.

It was a bedraggled little group that eventually knocked on the Dolls' House door.

Matilda began lessons in the nursery. She used the dolls' counting frame to teach sums. But the Rockery Mice were much more interested in the dolls' toys. Soon these were all over the floor.

Matilda decided to try cookery instead. She took the little mice down to the kitchen where George was in charge of lessons. But he couldn't find enough pots and pans for each mouse so he started an art lesson.

The little mice loved it. They did bubble painting and paw printing using berry jam. When Matilda returned she found George looking very hot and bothered and all the mice covered in jam.

George also taught the little mice to read, using scraps of paper that he collected from the dustbins. Soon they knew all the words on the labels of baked beans tins, crisps packets and sweet wrappers.

They learned their letters from newspaper that had been wrapped round fish and chips.

Matilda was now happy again and pleased with her school. But George thought the mice should learn more about the plants, flowers and insects outside. Helped by the older mice, he built a twig shelter beside the Dolls' House where they could have nature study lessons.

When ladybirds came in, the mice did sums by counting their spots. But when the ladybirds got hungry they would wander off to find new leaves to eat and then the sums were all wrong!

Sometimes a group of friendly worms appeared and curved themselves into letter shapes so the mice could practise their writing.

And once a spider showed them how to weave a web but when the little mice tried to copy it with cotton thread they got terribly tangled up.

During lessons in the shelter, the mice were always very quiet, in case the cat should hear them. But one day Bramble got up during a nature lesson and sang a song he had made up about a bee. It was such a lovely song that Matilda didn't like to stop him but as his little voice rose higher and higher, what she had always dreaded happened. With a crash and a growl the cat was among them!

The terrified mice scurried away in all directions but poor Bramble was caught! Matilda and Fergus hid nearby, staring in horror.

George grabbed a stick. 'Pull Bramble away at the first chance,' he whispered to Matilda.

She nodded, trembling. 'Oh, do be careful,' she squeaked.

George puffed up his chest and strode out in front of the cat, brandishing his stick and squeaking loudly. It had the right effect. The cat's eyes turned on him. With a snarl she sprang forward, releasing Bramble.

As George danced and dived about in front of the furious cat, Matilda crept out of her hiding place. Then George hit the cat's whiskers with his stick. Spitting and yowling, the cat pounced.

Matilda rushed forward and dragged Bramble away.

But George had tripped and dropped his stick. The cat's claw caught his stripey suit and flicked him in the air. George caught a glimpse of snapping yellow teeth as he fell, bruised and exhausted, into a bush.

He couldn't hear the cat now, but he knew she was still crouched in the bushes, waiting for him. Out of the corner of his eye, he saw a familiar sight – the dustbin! Gathering all his strength, George made a dash for it, but the cat was already there!

Now she fancied a game. She chased poor George round and round the dustbin. Then, for fun, she jumped up on top of it to dive down on him. But the dustbin lid wasn't fixed on tightly. As the cat sprang up, it tipped and the whole bin crashed down. The noise brought the cat's owner to the kitchen door and she was told crossly to go inside.

George lay, safe, but shaking with fright under the dustbin lid. His body was aching with pain from his bruises.

But even as he lay there, a smile spread slowly across his battered face, for out of the dustbin had tumbled something truly wonderful!

When George felt stronger, he made his way cautiously back
along the flower bed to the Dolls' House. Long before he got
there, however, he heard familiar squeaks and through the ivy
rushed his anxious family.

They greeted him with tears of joy and relief. Matilda hugged
George and then led him to see poor Bramble, who had now
recovered a little from his terrible experience. He was in the
nursery, sipping tea while Lobelia fussed round, bandaging
his cuts.

For Matilda the nightmare was not yet over. When she was alone again with George there was a knock at the door. Outside was a small group of the older Rockery Mice. News of the disaster had reached their parents and the little mice had been forbidden to return to school. The journey would be too dangerous now the cat knew what they were doing.

Matilda wept. The school would have to close.

To Matilda's surprise, George said nothing. He just smiled mysteriously, handed some strong rope to the Rockery Mice, and told them all to follow him.

When they got to the dustbin, George pushed aside some apple peelings, lifted up a paper bag and stood back proudly to show Matilda his find.

'It's a new school,' he announced happily. 'A floating school!'

At dawn the mice worked hard to drag the toy Noah's Ark to the pond and anchor it securely. They set to, to make paddles and seats for the inside.

They painted pictures for the walls and packed food into the cupboards. There was a peg for each little mouse to hang up its life jacket, and lockers for their pens and paper.

When the floating school was ready, the proud mice rowed it across the pond to show their parents and collect the pupils for the first lessons aboard the Ark.

For George and Matilda it was a dream come true. Now the mice could add pond life to their list of things to study and Fergus promised to start swimming lessons.

But best of all, the cat never interrupted them again, because, of course, cats hate getting their paws wet!